Old MacDonald had a Zoo

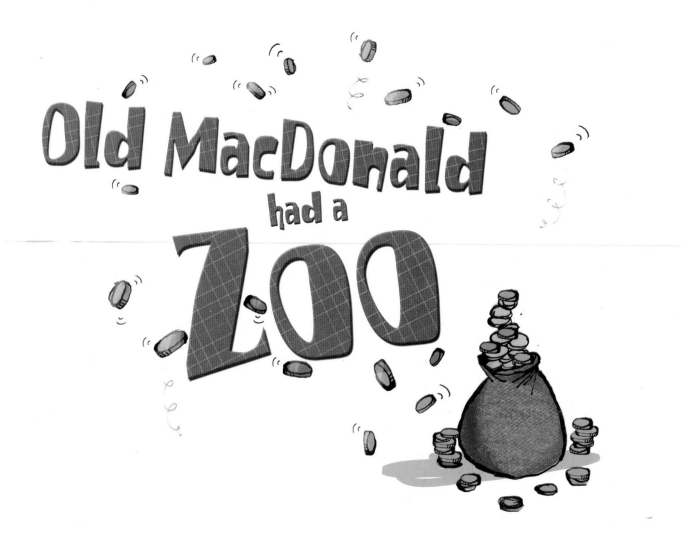

OLD MACDONALD WINS LOTTERY

An elderly farmer has won one million gold coins on the lottery. Mr Old MacDonald, of MacDonald's Farm, said: "I just need to find the right thing to spend it on now!"

ZOOKEEPER MISSING

Local zookeeper, Mr Arthur Kipper is missing. His boots were found in the penguin pool, his torn trousers in the lion cage and his hat and shirt in the monkey enclosure.

ZOO FOR SALE

The City Zoo has come up for sale. Buyers should be aware that the zoo is in need of safety improvements, including electric fences and dinosaur-strength tranquilisers. The asking price is one million gold coins, a bargain for any animal lover.

For Tom - Ooo! Ooo!
C.J. xxxxx

For Curtis, with love
T.M.

First published in Great Britain 2014
by Egmont UK Limited
This edition published 2019 by Dean,
an imprint of Egmont UK Limited,
The Yellow Building, 1 Nicholas Road,
London W11 4AN
www.egmont.co.uk

Text copyright © Curtis Jobling 2014
Illustrations copyright © Tom McLaughlin 2014
Curtis Jobling and Tom McLaughlin
have asserted their moral rights.

ISBN 978 0 6035 7768 0
70751/001

Printed in Malaysia

A CIP catalogue record for this title
is available from the British Library.

Curtis Jobling & Tom McLaughlin

Old MacDonald had a Zoo

DEAN

Gift Shop

EXIT

Old MacDonald had a zoo,

ee-i-ee-i-oh!

And in that zoo he had some **monkeys**,
ee-i-ee-i-oh!
With an **OOO OOO** here
and an **OOO OOO** there,

here an **OOO**,
there an **OOO**,
everywhere an
OOO OOO.

Old MacDonald had a zoo,
ee-i-ee-i-oh!

And in that zoo he had some **penguins**,
ee-i-ee-i-oh!
With a **HONK HONK** here
and a **HONK HONK** there,

here a **HONK**,
there a **HONK**,

everywhere a
HONK HONK.

Old MacDonald had a zoo, **ee-i-ee-i-oh!**

And in that zoo
he had a snake,
ee-i-ee-i-oh!
With a **HISS HISS** here .. and a **HISS HISS** there,
here a **HISS**,
there a **HISS**,

everywhere a **HISS HISS.**

Old MacDonald had a zoo,
ee-i-ee-i-oh!

And in that zoo
he had some **wolves**,
ee-i-ee-i-oh!

With a **HOWL HOWL** here
and a **HOWL HOWL** there,
here a **HOWL**, there a **HOWL**,

And in that zoo he had some **vultures,**

ee-i-ee-i-oh!

with a **KAW KAW** here
and a **KAW KAW** there,
here a **KAW,** there a **KAW,**
everywhere a **KAW KAW.**

Old MacDonald had a zoo,

ee-i-ee-i-oh!

And in that zoo he had some crocodiles,
ee-i-ee-i-oh!
With a **SNAP SNAP** here
and a **SNAP SNAP** there,

here a **SNAP**,
there a **SNAP**,
everywhere a
SNAP SNAP.

everywhere a
HOWL HOWL.

Old MacDonald
had a zoo,
ee-i-ee-i-oh!

Old MacDonald had a zoo, **ee-i-ee-i-oh!**

And in that zoo he had a lion,
ee-i-ee-i-oh!

With a
ROAR ROAR
here and a
ROAR ROAR
there,

here a **ROAR**,
there a **ROAR**,
everywhere a
ROAR ROAR.

Old MacDonald had a zoo, **ee-i-ee-i-oh!**

And in that zoo he had an elephant, **ee-i-ee-i-oh!**

With a **STOMP STOMP** here

and a **STOMP STOMP** there,

here a **STOMP,**
there a **STOMP,**

Gift
Shop

everywhere a
**STOMP
STOMP.**

Old MacDonald had a . . .